# BEAUTIFUL

Stacy McAnulty

ILLUSTRATED BY
Joanne Lew-Vriethoff

SCHOLASTIC INC.

ISBN 978-1-338-15200-5

12 11 10                                                                          20 21 22

Printed in the U.S.A.                                    40

First Scholastic printing, January 2017

Designed by T.L. Bonaddio
Edited by Lisa Cheng
Typography: Elsie, Close, and Daft Brush

For PAIGE and ELLERIE—AUNT STACY

For MAX WU YEN,
my baby girl, my inspiration—J.L.V.

# Beautiful girls . . .

. . . have the perfect look.

Beautiful girls move gracefully.

And light up every room.

Beautiful girls know all about makeup.

And have a smart style.

Beautiful girls smile sweetly.

And keep their hair properly in place.

Beautiful girls smell like flowers.

And sound like songbirds.

Beautiful girls love to look in the mirror.

And to spend time with beautiful people.

Beautiful girls deserve compliments.

Because they make the world . . .

BEAUTIFUL